THE
SHEPHERD'S SONG
~ THE TWENTY-THIRD PSALM ~

PICTURES BY JULIA MINER

DIAL BOOKS FOR YOUNG READERS NEW YORK

Published by Dial Books for Young Readers
A Division of Penguin Books USA Inc.
375 Hudson Street
New York, New York 10014

Library of Congress Cataloging in Publication Data
Bible. O.T. Psalms XXIII. English. Authorized.
The shepherd's song : the twenty-third psalm/
pictures by Julia Miner.—1st ed.   p. cm.
Summary: The text of the twenty-third psalm is illustrated
with scenes depicting a shepherd family.
ISBN 0-8037-1196-4
[1. Psalms.]   I. Miner, Julia, ill. II. Title.
BS1450 23rd 1986a   223'.2052034—dc20   91-31067   CIP   AC

The full-color paintings were rendered in pastels.

For Sara, John, and Ilse

The Lord is my shepherd;

I shall not want.

He maketh me
to lie down in green pastures:

he leadeth me
beside the still waters.

He restoreth my soul:

he leadeth me
in the paths of righteousness

for his name's sake.

Yea,
though I walk
through the valley
of the shadow of death,

thy rod and thy staff
they comfort me.

Thou preparest a table before me

in the presence

of mine enemies:

thou anointest my head with oil;
my cup runneth over.

Surely goodness and mercy shall follow me
all the days of my life:

and I will dwell
in the house of the Lord
for ever.

David, the psalmist, was a courageous shepherd boy who would later become a mighty king of Israel. While watching his sheep in the hills of Judea, he composed songs about God's watchful protection. His beautiful music became so well known that one time when King Saul was troubled, he sent for David. Listening to the young shepherd boy's music, the king soon felt refreshed and well. When we read David's poetry in the Book of Psalms, we too sense a protecting, calming presence.

The Twenty-third Psalm's message of complete trust rewarded by steadfast love and protection is familiar to a shepherd. I realized this when I met a dedicated shepherdess who owned and ran a farm near my former home in Massachusetts; I saw firsthand the constant care that raising sheep demands. Her meadows, ewes, and new lambs inspired the first sketches for *The Shepherd's Song*. Images of sheepherders following traditions similar to those in Biblical times came from my travels in the Greek Islands, where I watched shepherd children moving their flocks through the mountains.

Each phrase of the psalm describes a different facet of sheep-herding and gives a new insight into the peace we feel when we are moving in accord with universal Love, which is mirrored in every creature. In *The Shepherd's Song* the parents, children, dog, and sheep are all shepherds in their own way. Even the landscape and other animals reflect safety and harmony when Love's presence is felt.